DETROIT PUBLIC LIBRARY

P9-DDM-174

CHASE BRANCH LIBRARY
17731 W. SEVEN MILE RD.
DETROIT, MI 48235

JUL   2007

CH

Also by Andrea Cheng
Marika
Honeysuckle House
The Lace Dowry
Eclipse

To Nicholas—A.C.

Text copyright © 2007 by Andrea Cheng
Illustrations copyright © 2007 by Ken Condon
All rights reserved
Printed in China
Designed by Helen Robinson
First edition

Library of Congress Cataloging-in-Publication Data
Cheng, Andrea.
Tire mountain / Andrea Cheng ;
illustrations by Ken Condon.
p. cm.
Summary: A young boy who lives in the inner city adjusts to the idea of moving
away by building a playground out of the old tires from his father's repair shop.
ISBN-13: 978-1-932425-60-4 (hardcover : alk. paper)
[1. Tires—Fiction. 2. Inner cities—Fiction. 3. Neighborhood—Fiction.] I. Condon, Ken, ill. II. Title.
PZ7.C41943Ti 2007
[E]—dc22   2006011988

BOYDS MILLS PRESS, INC.
815 Church Street
Honesdale, Pennsylvania 18431

TIRE MOUNTAIN

Andrea Cheng

ILLUSTRATIONS BY **Ken Condon**

BOYDS MILLS PRESS
Honesdale, Pennsylvania

Mama's tired of cars coming and going and the smell of rubber all around.

"William," she tells Dad, "we are absolutely wallowing in tires."
But we're lucky to have our very own shop right next to our
house. Dad can change a tire faster than I can say *Aaron Jacob
Johnson*, and I have a tire mountain that gets taller every day.

At night, Dad locks the door of our shop. We climb up Tire Mountain
and watch the cars drive past. "Why does Mama want to move?" I ask.
A car with the radio blaring stops at the light. "Mama wants
someplace clean and beautiful for you to play," Dad says softly.
"It's beautiful here," I whisper, watching the taillights fade in the fog.

In the morning, Mama is looking at a pamphlet of houses for sale. What if she finds one so far from our shop that I can't walk over? I slip out the back door.

Mist is rising and Mr. Lumsfield is sweeping up the garbage in the empty lot. I push our sign out like I do every morning. A car with a flat tire pulls up and Dad is ready. He tosses the old tire to me and I push it to the top of my pile. Now my mountain is taller than it's ever been, higher even than the brown wooden fence.

On the other side, Miss Mattie is carrying stones in a wheelbarrow. Her eyes catch mine.

"I might be getting too old for this, Aaron," she says, dumping the stones.

"What are you making?" I ask.

She takes small black seeds out of her apron pocket. "A four o'clock garden. My husband used to grow these flowers all over the yard."

"Miss Mattie, my mama wants to move," I say.

Miss Mattie sets a stone in place. "That so?" She wipes
her forehead with the back of her hand. "You know, Aaron,
before you were born, this corner was neat as a pin."

I look around. "It's still a good corner," I say.

"Aaron," Dad calls. He has more tires for me. I drag them slowly up the steep sides of my mountain. When Mama comes home, she'll say to Dad, *William, these tires have to go.* Once I asked her if I could take my mountain to a new house. "Mountains do not move, Aaron," she said.

Heat waves rise from the blacktop. The smoke from S&S Barbeque stings my eyes. Miss Mattie leans on her shovel. "There was once a playground in that empty lot," she says. Then she heads down the driveway with her wheelbarrow.

At dinner, Mama shows us three houses she's circled. "I like this one the best." She points to a brick one with white trim.

"I hate it," I say.

"Aaron," Dad says in his warning voice.

I want to snatch that pamphlet with its perfect houses and tear it into a thousand pieces, but instead I run into my room and shut the door.

That night Mama and Dad are talking so loud. Mama says,
"It's time. We've saved long enough. I already looked at the
perfect house. Think about Aaron."
I cover my head with my pillow so I can't hear anymore.

Soon as I push our sign out in the morning, Miss Mattie's granddaughter, Candace, is there. "Play with me," she begs, grabbing my arm.

We stack tires and hide inside. We roll them down the slope. We make an obstacle course. At noon, she goes home for lunch. I climb up Tire Mountain and look across at the empty lot. I see the perfect spot for a tire swing in the catalpa tree.

Dad has some rope in the back of his pickup truck, but the first branch of the catalpa is way above my head. I stack six tires like a step stool, and finally I get the rope around the lowest branch. Just before dinnertime, the tire swing is ready. Candace is the first to try it out.

In the morning, I borrow Miss Mattie's wheelbarrow to make a tire garden. Two teenagers are watching.

"Think you're a farmer?" one asks.

I feel my throat swell.

"He grows tires," the other one says.

My hands tremble and I let go of one handle of the
wheelbarrow. It wobbles and tips, and most of the dirt spills
out. The boys laugh. I want to run back home and crawl into
a dark tire cave where they'll never find me. I take a deep
breath, set the wheelbarrow up, and shovel the dirt back in.

By the end of the week, the playground has two tire gardens, a tire swing, a tire tunnel, and a tire sandbox. Miss Mattie's son is bringing some sand tomorrow. Mr. Lumsfield knows a man who has a tire shredder so we can put rubber mulch under the swing.

Candace comes every day to play. And a boy and his cousin from around the block. And a mother with her baby in a stroller. Sometimes those teenagers stand on the corner, watching.

Every morning I water the seeds. Soon small
green shoots are sticking up all over. "How long
until we see the flowers?" I ask Miss Mattie.
"About the middle of June, I do recall."
"I might be gone by then," I say.

"Then I'll come get you," Miss Mattie says.

It's so hot that the tar melts on the side of the street.
We take to watering twice a day. Then one morning I see a
single bright pink blossom. By the end of the week there are
white and yellow and pink four o'clocks all around.

That night, Dad and I sit on top of Tire Mountain. We see Mama inside,
looking at her pamphlet again. Then she comes out and looks around.
"Looks to me like you've made your own park right here, Aaron Jacob," she
says. Mama folds the pamphlet and uses it like a fan.

I see the moonlight on her face. "When we do move, some day, do you
think we could take a tire?" I swallow hard. "To make a tire swing?"

Mama pulls me close. "That could be arranged."

The moon is shining big behind the catalpa, lighting up those
four o'clocks. But the playground looks a little empty.

"It still needs something," I say.

"You think?" Mama asks.

"How about a pretend car right in the middle," I suggest.

Miss Mattie joins us outside. "My husband had some old car parts in
the basement. I bet I could get those two teenagers to haul them up."

"Those mean boys?" I ask.

Miss Mattie nods. "They'll come around."

"Is there a steering wheel down there?" I ask.

"I believe there is."

"We could use real tires for the wheels," I say.

"Looks like Tire Mountain will be about gone," Dad says.

"We can put the new flat tires in the playground and make a mountain there," I say, smiling at Mama in the dark.